For Malcolm, with love

First published 2005 by Walker Books Ltd
87 Vauxhall Walk, London SE11 5HJ

This edition published 2006

2 4 6 8 10 9 7 5 3 1

© 2005 Sarah McMenemy

The right of Sarah McMenemy to be identified as author/illustrator
of this work has been asserted by her in accordance with
the Copyright, Designs and Patents Act 1988

This book has been typeset in Americana

Printed in Singapore

British Library Cataloguing in Publication Data:
a catalogue record for this book is available from the British Library

ISBN-13: 978-1-4063-0143-4
ISBN-10: 1-4063-0143-4

www.walkerbooks.co.uk

WALKER BOOKS
AND SUBSIDIARIES
LONDON · BOSTON · SYDNEY · AUCKLAND

Jack's New Boat

Sarah McMenemy

JACK went to stay with
his Uncle Jim for a holiday.
Uncle Jim was a sailor.
He had made Jack a boat.
Jack loved his boat – he wanted
to sail it straight away.

"Can we go and sail my
boat now?" asked Jack.

"We'd better wait.
It looks as if a storm
is coming,"
said Uncle Jim.
"Those waves would
sweep your boat out
to sea."

But the stormy weather only got worse.

Each morning Jack asked, "Please can I sail my boat today?"

And each time Uncle Jim replied, "All the big boats are in harbour today, Jack. Let's wait for a calmer sea."

All Jack
could think
about was
sailing his
new boat.

But each day
was windy
and wet ...

and the sea still crashed against the shore.

Jack thought he would burst
if he didn't sail his boat soon.

But still the rain
came down.

Until at last ...

it stopped!

Jack could wait
no longer.

He picked up
his boat and ran
down to the beach.

The waves
were still
very big.

I'll just hold it
at the edge of
the water,
thought
Jack.

He watched
it bobbing
up
and down.

I'll just let it go
for a moment...

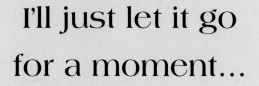

"Not
too far!"
he called.

But the boat drifted further
and further out to sea.
"Come back! Don't go!"
cried Jack,

as the boat tipped
and disappeared beneath
a giant wave.

"Uncle Jim, Uncle Jim!"
cried Jack.
"I've lost my boat – a big
wave took my boat!"

"Let's go and see,"
said Uncle Jim.

They searched up and down the beach
for hours, but they couldn't find anything.

"It's getting dark," said Uncle Jim. "Let's go home
now. We'll look again in the morning."

but they couldn't find the boat anywhere.

They searched again along the beach ...

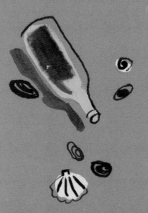

The next morning was bright and sunny. It made Jack feel hopeful.

Then Jack saw something red ...

but it wasn't his boat.

"I wish I'd waited for the weather to change," Jack said sadly.

"Do you think we'll ever
find my boat?" asked Jack.
"I don't know," said Uncle Jim.
"I hope so."

"Let's do something else
for a while to cheer ourselves up," he said.
"Let's go and look at the big boats in the harbour."

Jack cheered
up when he saw
all the colourful boats.

He shouted out each colour as he passed.

"Green, white, orange, yellow, green, blue, yellow, red... RED!"

Jack ran to look.

"It's my boat!" he shouted.

"I've found
my boat!"

"Can we mend it?"

"Of course,"
said Uncle Jim.
"We'll make her
seaworthy again."

And that's just what
they did.

WALKER BOOKS is the world's leading independent publisher of children's books. Working with the best authors and illustrators we create books for all ages, from babies to teenagers – books your child will grow up with and always remember. So…

FOR THE BEST CHILDREN'S BOOKS, LOOK FOR THE BEAR